Shadows Across Water
A Novella in Four Parts, by: Alexandre Kelsick

PART ONE: The Players

PART TWO: Master of Forms

12) Hubris

13) Nietzsche's Dance

PART THREE: Contact

INTERLUDE

PART Four: The Turning

PART ONE:
<u>The Players</u>

In and out,
Above, about, below,
'Tis nothing but a magic shadow-
show
Play'd in a box whose candle is the
sun
'Round which phantom figures
come and go
(Omar Khayyam)

Chapter One:
Heidi

In the autumn of 1939, a strikingly beautiful woman, Heidi Braun, made her way home in the German town of Freiburg. She was tall, with a slim figure and high cheek-bones, blonde hair cut short, piercing blue eyes, and wore very little make-up: dark-red lipstick to accentuate her sensual mouth, and eye-liner. Her dress was bohemian: long flowing lines, and autumn colours.

Along with most other Germans, Heidi had been swept up in the tide of Nazism. Unlike most Germans, she was not an ardent follower of Hitler. She had had the occasion to see him deliver a speech in Berlin, and the sheer intensity of the man had struck her as somewhat neurotic. But she was an opportunist, and a nihilist: she paid homage to nothing earthly. And yet she was capable of love, in her own reserved way. Above all, she was an individual.

She had taken a degree at the University of Freiburg in French literature, and was still without a job after many months of searching. In her early twenties, intelligent, from a family of some means and with a sense of adventure, she had therefore been flattered when a Gestapo agent had approached her one day, in Freiburg, and offered her the possibility of working for the Reich as an operative. She was aware that women were sometimes used to get information by seducing important men, and this did not bother her in the least. She rather liked the idea of espionage, and from the pictures she had seen of her target, Garay, as was his name, was not an unattractive man. The physical aspect would be easy enough. In any case, she did not have to pretend to be someone else. She would be herself, Heidi Braun, and all she had to do was study French literature at the Sorbonne while eliciting information from Garay.

At their last meeting, after a lengthy period of clandestine psychological and physical training, some of which had occurred in Freiburg but most of it in Berlin, Heidi's commanding officer, a reticent fellow with a sallow complexion named 'Klaus' (Heidi suspected that this was not his real name), had told her that she was to leave for France within the month. The day after tomorrow, in fact. September 22nd . Now all she had to do was to finish preparing herself mentally for the task at hand. She had been doing so by diminishing her contact with friends in Freiburg, giving herself time to be alone and to focus. She had ended the relationship she was having with a young professor of philology, Franz. She had enjoyed his company, but she would not miss him.

Nor would she miss Freiburg. Not for the moment, anyhow. She had enjoyed her last look at it today, and, yes, it was a charming town, but after five years as a student here she was ready to move on to something more cosmopolitan.

Heidi had been studying the dossier that Klaus had supplied her with: Garay's childhood in the south-west of France, his upbringing in a wealthy Basque family, his studies in law in Paris, his marriage to an aristocrat, and his path towards the political career that was now his life as an important figure in the Ministry of Foreign Affairs. She rather liked the profile of the man: a strong, independent type who was ambitious and ruthless in his pursuit of power. She would have little trouble seducing him, especially if the Gestapo were right about his taste for beautiful women. Heidi was intensely aware of her own beauty, and like most beautiful women, had learned at an early age how to use it to get what she wanted.

The plan was simple. The gestapo knew that Garay met often with a professor of philosophy, Gilbert Marcel, at a café called *La Scene*. Heidi was to enroll in Marcel's course, and then use him to get at Garay. She would wait for the appropriate moment at the café before trying to connect with the two men.

Heidi looked at the calendar on her wall. The 22nd was a Friday. She would take the train to Berlin, and then from there go directly to Paris. She had better finish packing. She had to give the keys to her apartment to her landlord, to whom she had already given a month's notice. She decided to pour herself a glass of wine before making the final preparations for her departure.

Chapter Two:
Crossing Paths

A lanky, red-headed man named Nicolas de Lastur meditated quietly over his mint tea, savouring its delicate scent. The café where he sat, *La Scene*, was typical; indeed, apart from its burgundy chairs and its distinct location in the lively heart of the 15th District, it could have been any other café in Paris: a zinc counter-top bar served as a central point of reference for tables and chairs jammed together, conversations mingling and betraying each other. In a corner, Nicolas looked on unobstrusively and listened. His posture reflected his love of existential certainty, his body serving as a platform from which to project his need for clarity onto the world: he sat upright in his chair, legs apart, leaning over the table slightly with his elbows planted firmly on it, holding the teacup in both hands. Occasionally the sole of his shoe scraped the ground in a long, thoughtful movement.

Several tables away sat two men drinking coffee. One of the men, with dark brown hair and a trim moustache, had handsome features: intense blue eyes set pleasantly wide apart, and a Roman nose dominating a generous mouth and strong chin. The man with him had a head of unruly blonde hair, and an unusual face whose expression inclined towards arrogance. His features were sharp, hawklike, his eyes dark and penetrating. A red scarf dangled loosely around his neck. Nicolas knew the man with the red scarf. Indeed, he knew him well. He was a professor of philosophy, Gilbert Marcel. Nicolas had taken a course with him on Nietzsche. Nicolas had enjoyed the course, especially appreciating Marcel's rich and compassionate humanism, and his scepticism of all grandiose claims for Truth. They had struck up a lively friendship ever since. Nicolas, who had been studying the two men intently, realised that Marcel was looking at him, and had recognised him. Marcel waved to him. Nicolas got up, and made his way towards their table.

'Hello, Nicolas! Good to see you! Please join us,' said Marcel warmly, as he shook hands with Nicolas. 'Let me introduce you. This is Jean Garay, a good friend of mine. Jean, this is Nicolas de Lastur, a doctoral student in philosophy at the Sorbonne with whom I have had the pleasure to work.'

'Good to meet you,' said Nicolas, and extended his hand to Garay, who shook it firmly.

And you,' said Garay, in a deep, resonant voice. 'Would you care for a coffee?'

'Yes, with pleasure.'

Garay caught the attention of the waiter with a wave of his hand, and ordered a coffee.

'Jean is originally from the Basque country. You're one of those mountain people, aren't you Jean?' said Marcel, a mischievous smile playing on his lips.

'Indeed,' replied Garay. He glanced at Nicolas in an attempt to gauge the situation, and satisfied that Nicolas and Marcel were more than mere acquaintances, he relaxed somewhat.

'Jean is from Uhart-Cizes in the Pyrennees-Atlantiques, just next to St. Jean Pied de Port, which I'm sure you've heard of, Nicolas,' Marcel continued, obviously enjoying the momentary discomfiture that he had caused his friend. 'But he now lives in Paris with his beautiful wife and children, and is deeply involved in politics. He is an aide to the Minister for Foreign Affairs. We were just talking about the situation in Europe. Jean has some interesting ideas on the threat Germany poses to France. You think that Hitler is a menace, isn't that right, Jean?'

'Well, if you insist Gilbert. But I'll commit to nothing,' said Garay, in an ironic tone, his hands resting on the table, palms down in tenacious repose.

Nicolas smiled. The two men were obviously good friends to be able to banter as they did, and to speak with such ease about topics that carried some weight. Many feared that war with Germany was imminent, and were already accusing France of not putting up enough opposition to fascism such as it had come to exist in Italy, Germany and Spain. Some were saying, in the face of the French government's repeated attempts to appease Hitler, that France would rather choose fascism over atheist communism. To support French foreign policy might therefore suggest a certain sympathy for fascism. If, that is, the critics of France were to be believed. On the other hand, to oppose French foreign policy was to take an anti-government stance, and if this was what Garay was doing, he was his staking political reputation on it.

"I have a question,' said Nicolas. 'Perhaps I should address it to Monsieur Garay. It's on the subject of Germany. I hope you don't mind?'

'Not at all,' replied Garay. 'Indeed, I seem to think of little else these days. As Gilbert is so quick to remind me.' Marcel smiled.

'What do you think, Monsieur, of Hitler's call for increased *lebensraum* for the German people? Does it not pose a threat to the peace in Europe? Don't you think that Hitler is likely to drag France and her allies into another conflict, perhaps even bigger than that of the Great War? Isn't fascism an abomination, what with all its talk about 'purity' and its hateful persecution of the Jews, and others? Shouldn't we be doing more to resist Hitler?'

'These are questions that are on everyone's minds these days,' replied Garay, with a certain gravity, folding his arms. 'Certainly it would seem, with the remilitarisation of Germany, and her alliance with the fascist armies of Italy and Spain, that war in Europe is imminent. Having annexed Austria and now wanting to do the same with Czechoslovakia, it is not at all clear that Hitler will stop there. He has often spoken of peace, but he clearly means to make Germany a great imperial power again. One can only hope that if German aggression does finally threaten the capitalist democracies of Western Europe, that France will be fully prepared to defend herself. With the aid, of course, of Great Britain. What is clear is that

France and England have no desire to go to war again, and will do everything within their power to appease Germany. I am not sure if this is the right policy. A preventive war might be better, stopping Germany before she becomes too strong. What is certain is that we live in dangerous times, and there is no telling how they will play themselves out. Not for the moment, anyhow.' Garay glanced at his watch. 'Ah. I'm afraid I have to rush off, gentlemen. A pleasure to have met you, Nicolas. I hope we can continue this conversation another time.' He quickly drank his coffee, put some coins on the table, and rose out of his seat.

'Gilbert, please excuse me. I have a meeting to go to that I almost forgot about. And then I am off to the mountains, where every bent philosopher searching for sanity should be. With no great effect, I'm sure.'

'Not at all,' said Marcel, laughing at Garay's tardy riposte, quite pleased that he had been able to touch a nerve, however lightly. He rose to shake Garay's hand. 'It's been a pleasure, as always , talking with you, Jean. I look forward to doing it again.'

'Me too. Bye for now.'

Garay shook hands with Nicolas, and walked briskly out of the café.

<u>Chaper Three</u>
Shadow Play

Nicolas and Marcel sat in silence, drinking their coffees.

'An interesting man, Garay. I enjoyed our brief conversation,' said Nicolas.

'Yes, Jean has a good mind, and a bright future ahead of him. If there is a future for French politicians, with Germany on the prowl again. This Hitler is up to no good, I'm afraid. Only time will tell how much havoc he intends to wreak. He hopes to be a great man, I fear, and like all such men he has, unfortunately, little grasp of his own insignificance. If only he knew himself as the shadow that he is.'

'How do you mean, exactly?'

'We are all really shadows, you know, Nicolas,' Marcel replied, his voice quiet but firm in the manner of one who is accustomed to explaining things. 'Indeed, we are shadows cast across water. And there is nothing more insubstantial than a shadow cast across water.'

'Yes, but …'

'No, wait. You will object that I reduce life to a metaphor. And you are right. Yet is life not like this? Think about it. We have become accustomed to seeing ourselves as thinking creatures of flesh and blood, walking in God's image. *We* cast shadows. But there is a sense also in which we are shadows cast by Being's light. Reality, Nicolas, is like a great, dynamic body of water, above which Being shines; and we are as shadows of Being reflected across reality, our fleshy existence deflecting the bright light of being: a light which limits what we can achieve in a play of shadows. We can only interpret the truth. If we realise that we are like shadows across water, we are likely to accept the relative insignificance of the shadow-play that is life. In this acceptance lies our recognition of the irony of existence. And by this I mean that life has no ultimate meaning, aside from the interpretive movement which resides in Being's shadow-play. And acceptance of this movement is for the better, I think. But it is not easy, you see, and we are often inspired to reject our nature as shadow, and we demand a narcissistic turn towards Being itself '

'This is Hitler's problem, then, thinking that he has discovered truth itself? You're saying that he has failed to admit that he is a mere shadow moving through dynamic truths, quite apart from Being *as such*?'

'Exactly. It is up to us what we shall make of life, Nicolas. We can choose to be ironic and to take meaning as it comes, and to laugh at the demand for the truth of Being itself; or we can become obsessed with that demand. If we choose to laugh, as ironists do, we accept the ambiguity of our fleshy existence, and come to terms with the shadows cast by Being's Light – a Light whose shadows are the truth of reality: *as reality is given to us by Being.* No light without shadow.' Marcel paused to fill a pipe that he had fished out of his pocket.

'Yes,' said Marcel, blowing blue smoke into the sky as his pipe came alive. 'Accepting the shadow means coming to terms with the fact that we are, ultimately, absurd creatures. *We are finite modifications of God's essence.* There is no Absolute Truth to human being. We are not God … If, on the other hand, we reject the condition of our existence, and aspire to the Fullness of Being, we become empty shadows cast across water, the meaning of our fragile lives devoured by an insatiable hunger for Truth. Hubris, I think, is the right word. Like Icarus who flew too close to the sun, we plummet to earth with scorched wings. The good, Being, is beyond us, you see. It is what we become when we die … if we have good karma, so to speak. Being is whole. We are finite modifications of its power. We are evil becoming good. We are all sinners.'

The two men fell silent again. It had started to rain. Marcel's hawklike features assumed an expression of intense focus as he reflected on the prospect of war. Nicolas sensed the older man's mood, and shared his concern. He watched as a flock of pigeons suddenly flew into the air, disturbed by a group of children returning home from school. He felt lightened by the children's carefree laughter as they experienced the peculiar delight of fluttering wings. Nicolas wished for a moment that he could return to the innocence of childhood, to its simplicity and naïve openness to life. Like Marcel, he had a premonition of dangerous and complex times ahead.

Chapter Four:
Complexity

Nicolas left Marcel at *La Scene*. He was tired and hungry. But the time had been well spent. It was always good to chat with Marcel, whose mind worked in fascinating ways. And it had been a stroke of good luck to have met Jean Garay, whose thoughts on the German threat confirmed Nicolas's own suspicions. Unfortunately there was nothing to be done about it. Better to concentrate on the moment, and let the future take care of itself. And so Nicolas turned his attention to what was happening around him as he made his way home.

Paris, the Great City, was winding down. It was a time of day that Nicolas knew well and liked best, a slowing down as people returned home from work or school. There was not much about Paris that Nicolas didn't know well. He had been born in the 16th District, to wealthy aristocratic parents, and had had an upbringing surrounded by books and classical music, occasionally spending time with his grandparents in the Swiss Alps. At an early age he had developed a passion for philosophy, a passion that had grown into an academic career. His parents still lived in the house in which Nicolas had grown up, his father a successful surgeon whose passion was tending roses, and his mother a classical pianist who complained that her husband's roses had long ago become the great love of his life.

Nicolas walked through the 15th District on his way home (he lived not far from the Eiffel Tower, on the *rue de Laos*), and the city continued to impress itself on him, as it had in *La Scene*: He was struck by the variety of people he encountered, of age, race, gender, nationality, shape, size, and humour. Arab shop-keepers sold their wares. Children skipped alongside their parents. Men and women exchanged inviting, hostile or disinterested looks. A fat orthodox Jew waddled along, muttering to himself. A north African sold his wares. A tall American spoke sternly to his young son, who, perhaps missing his friends back home, was upset, and obviously could not care less that he was in one of the most beautiful cities of the world.

The complexity of Parisian society never grew dull for Nicolas, and he wondered what the Nazis were thinking when they talked about racial purity. Fascism was expressing itself in Germany as the agitation of a people finding, or thinking itself, adrift in pollution. In the face of this drift, Germans were demanding unity, and purity. Hitler was making sure that, through Nazism, Germans were obliged to simplify and consolidate life by getting rid of all that might be deemed strange, dirty, impure: already there were signs that he wanted to do away with the insane, the physically disabled, homosexuals, Gypsies, and, of course, the Jews. One need only read *Mein Kampf* to understand what Hitler meant to do.

Wasn't it the complexity of life that made it interesting, thought Nicolas? Turning onto the *Boulevard de Grenelle*, he meandered through an open-air market typical of Paris. It was still raining, and there was a sea of umbrellas as far as the eye could see. The market thronged with people. It possessed its own rhythms, of buying and selling, looking, comparing, with a myriad of things on offer: an infinite variety of cheese, vegetables, all sorts of meats, fish, clothes, jewellery, fruit, books, antique furniture, cutlery, sweets and desserts, amongst other things. Nicolas moved quickly and quietly, as one who is accustomed to walking through crowded urban spaces, focussed on the general movement of things and people around him. He felt the situation: he listened, he observed, he surreptitiously touched passers-by and caressed objects for sale, he tasted the air, and he smelled the wonderful odours of fresh herbs and the less attractive odour of human sweat.

Still feeling hungry and somewhat tired, and having been drenched by the rain (he did not have an umbrella), Nicolas stopped only to buy a bottle of wine before continuing on his way home. He decided on a bottle of Bordeaux, paid for it, and slipped it into his satchel.

Chapter Five:
Guernica

Nicolas let himself into his one-bedroom flat, and saw his lover Katya reading a journal.

'My god, you're soaking wet,' exclaimed Katya when she looked up and saw him, 'You got caught in the rain. Here, let me have your coat.'

'Thanks. How goes it?' Nicolas asked.

'I've been reading about Picasso's *Guernica*,' said Katya. You know, the horror of it all. Here is how one political commentator describes it: *'screams and disembodied voices with distorted faces. Not voices, really. More like tonalities bringing to mind archetypal spirits. Dark places full of destruction and perversity. An edge cutting endlessly into reality. A sexual grimace lost somewhere in the folds of severed flesh. A hacking, piercing, exploding truth to it all ... a demonic play of shadow and light ... a sign, perhaps, of things to come.'*

Nicolas nodded with a sad intensity. Indeed, a sign of things to come ...

Chapter Six:
Christ and the Wolf

Having made love, Nicolas and Katya lay in each other's arms, whispering secrets in each other's ears. Gently, they fell asleep. Gently, Nicolas' consciousness metamorphosed as he drifted deeper into sleep, and into the realm of dreams.

That night Nicolas had a vision within a dream: Christ running naked alongside a wolf in the depth of an Arctic winter, on a clear, sunny day. The god, with long flowing hair, and a body hardened by years of carpentry, running barefoot across snow and ice, muscles flexing, his breath frosty in the wind, his eyes fixed on an indefinite point on the horizon. His stride is beautiful to watch, rhythmic, like a dancer, his entire being focussed absolutely on running, on sharing the rhythm of the moment with the great grey wolf who runs with him. He gives no sign of feeling the cold because he is a supernatural being, one for whom freezing temperatures are a matter of habit. He is the incarnation of purity. At his side, the wolf, a creature driven by instinct, a social being whose predatory aspect moves in rhythm with the natural flow of things: its breath, also frosty in the wind, its shoulders pumping like pistons, grey fur beautiful to the eye, its eyes bright with expression.

Nicolas awoke suddenly, emerging from the dream-world abruptly, his eyes wide open. His dream still fully upon him, he lay quietly, allowing its sensations, colours and emotions to register fully in his mind. Katya's breathing was the only sound which disturbed the delicate stillness of the night. He lay awake for a long time, fighting off sleep, not wanting to let go of the pulsating energy which flowed through him as he reflected upon Christ and the wolf. Gradually he drifted into sleep again, but with the feeling of having experienced something of vital, life-transforming importance ….

Chapter Seven:
Lovers

Nicolas got up early, in time to watch the sun rise. The sky was clear, promising to become a bright blue. He sat in the kitchen, eating a simple breakfast: a croissant with butter and jam, and a cup of coffee. The apartment was quiet. Nicolas had already been up for about an hour when Katya managed to drag herself out of bed. A door opened, and he heard her making her way to the kitchen. A few moments later, she emerged, naked, her nipples firm, her pubic hair a gentle tangle, her hair wrapped in a towel.

'Good morning!' she said, leaning to kiss Nicolas on the forehead.

'Hello, Sleep well?'

'Yep. And you?'

'Yes. I had a strange dream, though. About Jesus Christ, of all things.

'Hmm. That's interesting. What was Christ doing?'

'Running. With a wolf.'

'Running with a wolf? Sounds Freudian, don't you think?'

'I don't know. Perhaps. I need to think about it. What are you up to today?'

'I've decided to stay here to work on my novel, if that's OK.'

'Yes, that's fine. Will you be here tonight?'

'I have an audition. It may be late before I'm finished.'

'An audition. Excellent !' While not writing, Katya aspired to be an actress in small theatres around Paris, taking work wherever she could find it, and so long as it interested her. Nicolas knew how important these auditions were for her. 'What's the play?'

'Shakespeare. Hamlet.'

'Ah. A fine play. "The play's the thing in which I'll catch the conscience of the king." I love that line. It seems to me to encapsulate a subtle truth about rebellion.'

'How so?'

'Well, you know, sleight of hand, and all that. Using fiction to get at fact.'

'Hmm.'

Nicolas finished his coffee. 'What part are you auditioning for?'

'I don't know yet. It's a wait and see thing.'

'Oh, OK. Listen, I've got to run. I've promised to meet Richard for a chat and lunch, and I'd better be leaving now or I'll be late.' He paused, and wiped a drop of water off Katya's brow. 'I enjoyed last night.'

'So did I. Tell you what. I'll come by after the audition. OK?'

Nicolas smiled. He had got the response he had hoped for. He kissed Katya, holding her head delicately between his hands. He cherished the charged sexual energy that had always been a part of their relationship, and which showed no signs of diminishing.

'See you later.'

'OK, see you.'

Chapter Eight:
Truth

Nicolas walked to his meeting with Richard. They had agreed to meet at Notre Dame, which was not too far away. Nicolas usually walked when going somewhere close by, preferring to avoid the metro whenever possible. Above ground, he felt more in touch with the city, in all its wonderful complexity.

The sun had risen high in the sky. It was a beautifully clear day, ideal for walking. Nicolas reflected on the day before, and wondered what sense he could make of it. It had been an unusually charged day: the chance encounter with Gilbert Marcel and Jean Garay, the spectre of war looming, the market-place, Picasso's Guernica, the dream about Christ and the wolf. His need for clarity was, as usual, pressing, and he felt within himself the urge to confront all of it, and make a definitive claim, about what he wasn't sure. About the Truth, perhaps? How could one get at 'the Truth?' And then he thought: what if one were to make no claim whatsoever about 'the Truth'? What was it that Marcel had said about shadows? Was it not dangerous to become obsessed with the Truth of Being?

What if one, in reflecting upon yesterday, were to embrace it not all at once, but rather as irony, at daybreak? A new day was dawning, and perhaps a different way of thinking should emerge with it.

It was not a question of becoming a sceptic, of denying that truth existed. One need not forsake clarity. To say, for instance, that sugar was sweet was a fact: it was trivially true. There were many such facts, and one could be clear about all of them. What was at issue for Nicolas was the idea of an all-embracing Truth, one that might, in axiomatic fashion, explain the very essence of reality. This sort of Truth paraded itself as a capitalised sovereign of being, as 'Truth of Being' pure and simple. Any theory which purported to explain reality in axiomatic fashion subscribed to this version of Truth. Whether it was Marxists claiming that all social evolution was caused by class conflict, or Hitler claiming that the destiny of humanity was to be dominated by a master race, there was a deadly seriousness about the business of Truth (of Being). This was what Marcel resisted, and Nicolas sympathised with him. How could one be – *not so serious?* How could one take things as they come, partially, and laugh? To not worry so much about Truth. Indeed, should one, as Marcel had suggested, bring ridicule upon Truth in ironic fashion? Nicolas had always been fascinated by irony. Irony in the sense, that is, of using humour and sarcasm so as to show up the discrepancy between the expected and actual state of affairs. It was a question of being able to mock the apparent fitness of things, as if everything should fit together to make up 'the Truth'.

As the sun continued to rise over Paris, Nicolas felt something within himself giving way to the world, in the face of which he was beginning to understand his relative insignificance. He focussed on the rhythm of his walking, running his fingers idly along a fence, peeling off bits of dried paint which had become detached from the steel. Walking always made thinking easier for him. For the moment Nicolas felt himself giving way before irony, and knew this giving way to be good. He was finding his place in the world, lightly, with a willingness to bring ridicule on Truth, as was the world finding its place in him.

Chapter 9:
Transcendence

Richard, an English seminarian in the Anglican Church, whose broad girth and wide shoulders reminded Nicolas of a medieval friar, was waiting for him near the entrance to Notre Dame. The two men had met during a course on Christian theology at the Sorbonne, and had quickly struck up a friendship. Richard had an agile mind, and Nicolas admired his ability to cut through academic dross to get at the heart of a difficult idea. He hoped that that same ability would be of some help to him today in making sense of his dream. As Nicolas approached, the two friends smiled at each other, and embraced.

'How are you, Richard?'

'Well. And you?'

'Well also. It's good to see you! You look more like a satisfied priest every time I see you! My god, what are they feeding you?'

Richard smiled. 'Actually, the food is awful,' he replied, calmly, but with a glint of good humour in his eyes. 'Shall we visit the cathedral?'

'Certainly. Notre Dame is always worth a visit.'

Walking towards the cathedral, the two friends fell silent, allowing the presence of Notre Dame to speak for itself. Nicolas adored Notre Dame, the impressive architecture of it, and the great statue of Charlemagne presiding over the entrance. The flying buttresses were magnificent, like giant wings of angels. Entering the monument, the two friends approached the central altar, and admired the surrounding altars, beautiful rose windows and majestic interior columns. The building was exquisite, beyond words, almost. For a moment, Nicolas imagined the cathedral at the height of Catholic influence, alive with priests, prayer, secrets and half-truths. The power of expression must have been formidable, indeed!

Leaving Notre dame, Nicolas and Richard made their way to a café just alongside, and ordered two beers.

'How are things at the seminary?' asked Nicolas.

'Oh, not bad,' replied Richard. 'The training is very rigorous.'

'I can imagine. What with all the courses you're taking, do you find time to meditate?'

'Oh, yes! Every day a portion of the schedule is devoted to prayer and meditation. And thank God for that, for it helps me to centre myself in the midst of a very busy schedule!'

'Listen,' said Nicolas, getting straight to the point. 'Perhaps you can help me solve a problem. I'm increasingly inclined to see the notion of the Truth of Being, the idea that there is an Absolute Explanation for reality, with an ironic eye. I had a dream last night, about Christ, and I must admit that, in all seriousness, Christian 'purity' still calls to me, despite my interest in irony. In fact the attraction is profound. You see, the problem is that there is something about Christian purity that strikes me as being 'True', in the absolute sense of the word. Can one strike a compromise between the two, between irony and Christian purity, do you think?'

'An interesting question,' replied Richard. 'I too think about purity a lot. You know, in the Church, priests are admitted sinners. But tell me about your dream. Can you describe it for me?'

Nicolas described the dream to Richard, as best he could, for it is not easy to convey the power of a vision in words.

'A demanding dream,' said Richard. 'I especially like the presence of the wolf. The wolf is simply what it is. It transcends good and evil in the banal sense of the terms, and reaches out to the divine figure of Christ. Purity here resides in simplicity: in motion, in rhythm, in a transformative movement that takes us beyond what is merely animal. The dream brings the animal, human and divine together, without negating what is animal. There is a strong sense of forgiveness in the vision, of all that is material. In fact, matter transcends itself, or is made to do so. Matter is laid bare in the form of the wolf, and transformed in the naked flesh of Christ, presented to the world in all his divine, dynamic beauty. And yet you insist on irony. Perhaps you insist too much?'

'What do you mean, 'too much'?'

'Well, perhaps your attraction to purity is strong enough to catapult you in the opposite direction, towards irony. Perhaps the problem resides not so much in the difference between the two sentiments, but in the desire that brings them together, and forces them apart. You may yet find a way for them to co-exist.'

'I hadn't thought of that,' admitted Nicolas. 'And yet, the two sentiments really are different, aren't they. Did not Christ, for his part, fit together with the wolf in an absolute sense, beyond the reach of all mockery? Can one win a fight in a seemingly hostile world without the motivating power, strength and beauty, of Christian purity? Purity is all about faith, redemption, and hope, while irony is all about poking fun at reality, being ironic about Truth with a capital 'T', not taking things so seriously. There are, there must be, different kinds of dreams, some more or less pure than others. I mean, I see your point about desire, but aren't you being a bit too abstract? Isn't there a concrete decision to be made about whether one pursues irony or purity? A decision reflected in the manner in which one chooses to live one's life?'

'No, it's not that easy,' replied Richard. 'Look at me! I've chosen to become a priest, but I don't ask God that my life be made pure. On the contrary, such a life would be, in the midst of all the impurities of the world, sheer anguish. But one can, and I certainly do, wish for moments of grace, of spiritual transcendence. This is what you experienced in your dream, my friend: a powerful moment of transcendence. For the moment, this moment, all I can say is: welcome back to earth, purity and all!'

Nicolas looked fondly at Richard's bright eyes, and laughed.

'OK, I'll think about what you've said. Would you like to have some lunch?'

'Yes, sure,' said Richard. Nicolas caught the waiter's attention, and the two friends ordered sandwiches.

Chapter 10:
Forgiveness

As he walked to the Sorbonne after having left Richard, Nicolas reflected on their conversation. He was inclined to accept Richard's reasoning. What he had experienced as 'Christian purity' was a moment of spiritual transcendence; or, better, a *movement* of transcendence: a *'transformative movement'*, as Richard had put it. This movement was not about Truth, Being, or Purity: it existed for itself, despite and *in relation with,* the impurities of the world. It made no absolute claim on reality. It was spiritual above all else. It placed reality in question, without insisting on the negation of that which it placed in question. In this sense, it was quite different to fascism, which, in its search for purity, lays claim to a Higher Truth, seeking to obliterate what it cannot control, what it deems inferior, impure.

Yes, one had to make room for different kinds of purity, for different aspirations. One could aspire to Purity in the dogmatic sense of wanting to do away with everything impure, as does fascism, or one might aspire to purity while being able to forgive the world for its lack of purity. Nicolas was sure as could be that his love of purity was not fascist, that it had nothing to do with Truth, and that it could indeed leave room for irony, even if the latter situated itself very much in the material world, in all its absurd partiality and impurity. There were perhaps different forms of purity, some gentle, some brutal, but it was the simpler, more forgiving sort, that was taking hold of Nicolas, which he saw reflected in his vision of Christ. Irony, for its part, was this side of spiritual purity: insofar as it resisted Truth, it had to do with the material world, and everything in it, that which purity transcended, and ultimately forgave for being merely biological. *In 'forgiveness' lay the divine meaning of the relation between purity and matter.*

Chapter 11:
Autumn Leaves

In the second week of November, 1939, Jean Garay walked at a brisk pace through the *Jardins Luxembourg* in Paris, on his way home from a parliamentary debate on Franco-German relations. The debate had come as a welcome change from his ordinary routine. He had made a point of being in parliament today because the French Foreign Minister had addressed France's position vis-à-vis Germany. Garay was an aide to the Foreign Minister in the Daladier government. He moved in circles of power, prestige, and social networking. He was an extrovert, and enjoyed the cut and thrust of debate, the movement of words and energy between individuals and groups, and the conflictual and synergistic exchange of ideas in the political arena.

Garay had grown up in the Pyrennees-Atlantiques, in the small Basque village of Uhart-Cizes. Born into a wealthy Basque family, he had had a privileged childhood, moving between the Pays Basque and Paris, and between France and Argentina, where his family owned property. Although first his legal and then his political career had brought him to Paris (he had frowned upon provincial politics early on), he still loved the mountains in which he grew up, and their environs. And with good reason, for anyone who has visited the southwest of France has experienced the beauty of it. There is the Basque coast, with the picturesque town of Biarritz upon whose shores the powerful waves of the Atlantic thunder home; and St. Jean de Luz, whose protected bay allows for pleasant and tranquil sea bathing. Uhart-Cize lies half an hour inland from Biarritz, to the south, very close to the Spanish border, its buildings with white walls, red shutters, and red-tiled roofs typical of the Pays-Basque. Nestled in the mountains, it is lush in the summer, and offers dazzling vistas of snow-capped peaks in the winters. Indeed, Garay had not really abandoned the Basque country, where he still kept close contact with friends and political allies. He still had the family home to go back to when he grew tired of Paris, a chateau built by his mother at the turn of the century. But the family also had other lodgings, and he sometimes secluded himself in a lodge high up in the mountains, where the sheep roam, writing, and pigeon-hunting during the season.

And yet, Garay spent most of his time in Paris. He had set his sights on national politics at an early age, in university, and had ruthlessly pursued his ambition to fruition. His social pedigree had of course helped him to get into the right schools and university, a necessity if one was to have access to the hierarchical circles of power that dominated France in the Third Republic. He had been careful to marry well, to Marianne, a French aristocrat quite a bit younger than himself. This helped allay doubts about his Basque identity: the Basques did, after all, have a reputation as being nationalistic, and their language was distinct from French. (Indeed, the Basque language is distinct from the family of Indo-European languages in general, making the Basques an especially unique people.) Garay had had two children with his wife, a boy and girl, and this completed his stature as a Frenchman worthy of trust and respect. That said, Garay's marriage did not prevent him from enjoying the company of other women, and he had quickly moved from one mistress to another during the five years that he had been married.

Garay stood still, and looked at the gardens around him. The trees were beautiful in autumn, their colour a reddish-gold, their branches beginning to show in stark relief against the blue sky where the foliage had left them. He kicked at the fallen leaves. He always enjoyed walking through the park, but especially at this time of year. There was a natural melancholy about autumn that spoke to the part of him which loved poetry. Autumn conveyed a sense of the inherent transience of things, their fragility. The mood fit well with the foreboding unease he felt about the German threat to France. He could not know that that threat was far more real and imminent than even he imagined, and that radical change would happen more quickly than he anticipated. Indeed, he was soon to be swept away by the most dangerous adventure of his life, like a leaf taken by an autumn wind and propelled skyward into the unknown.

Part Two:
<u>Master of Forms</u>

Hamlet: ... there are many confines, wards, and dungeons, Denmark being one o'th'worst

Rosencrantz: We think not so, my lord.

Hamlet: Why , then 'tis none to you. For there is nothing good or bad but thinking makes it so. To me it is a prison.

Rosencrantz: Why, then your ambitions makes it one. 'Tis too narrow for your mind.

Hamlet: O God, I could be bounded in a nutshell and count my self a king of infinite space, were it not that I have bad dreams

Guildenstern: which dreams indeed are ambition. For the very substance of the ambitious is merely the shadow of a dream.

Hamlet: a dream itself is but a shadow.

Rosencrantz: Truly, and I hold ambition of so airy and light a quality that it is but a shadow's shadow.

Hamlet: Then our beggars bodies, and our monarchs and outstretched heroes the beggar's shadows ....

***

Thoughts are the shadows of our sensations – always darker, emptier, simpler than these (Friedrich Nietzsche)

Chapter 12:
Hubris

There are some men who believe themselves destined for greatness, and whose vision of Truth, however skewed, leaves an indelible mark on the world. Adolf Hitler was one such man. In the Spring of 1938, we find Hitler pacing back and forth in his study in Berlin.

Finally, thought Hitler, he had realised what he had so long dreamed of! Austria, his birth-place, was now a part of the Reich, and Czechoslovakia must soon follow. Germany was being united as never before since 1914, and he could sense the inevitability of his own greatness. Was he not the one who had led Germany to economic revival, and rebuilt her armed forces, making her into a power once again to be reckoned with? Yes, the time had come for Germans to heed destiny's call, to become the great nation that they had always been meant to be, and to dominate Europe.

The Third Reich would last a thousand years! Hitler felt brazen power flowing through him, and could only marvel at the lack of resistance being offered by the western allies, France and

England. They obviously had little appreciation for the sheer magic of German theatre, set on a grand, cosmic scale.

Of course, Hitler reminded himself, one could not take wholly seriously what was in part so obviously theatrical. Leave it to the party cadre to invest magic with belief. He could only smile at the inspiration with which their faces glowed. That was the key: that they should *believe* in the sanctity of Germany's mission, in her flags, and in her blood oaths. That they should believe themselves pure Aryans, with every right to rule the world, this was important. That they should know themselves as actors on history's stage, as wholly insignificant servants of his mission, this was not important. In fact, they must not know, if they were to be effective agents of his will, he, their Absolute Lord, their Fuhrer. Germans must believe to the point of death in the role they were to play. He could only smile at their innocence and trust. That he should lead, and make of them instruments of his will, so it must be. Only he had the foresight and strength of will to forge Germany's future as one would a sword of pure steel, all the better to cut through the racial mediocrity that threatened to dominate the world. The belief of the German masses in their purity must become his will made pure. Here lay the true meaning of the word 'pure' for the Nazi party: the unbending will of the Fuhrer, his vision of Being made reality. *He was Germany's Truth. He was the sun around which the world must one day revolve, and all he deemed impure had to be annihilated.* Any other meaning of the word 'pure' was based on mere belief and symbolism, and could only lead to its higher, truer meaning, incarnated in the figure of the One, Hitler. If he had an ideology, about racial purity and the inevitability of German greatness, it was rooted in one single Truth: that he was the Truth of his times set in motion, the unstoppable, Nietzschean will to power. He was the Chosen One, the Master of Forms. Being itself.

Hitler laughed. That destiny should have put him where he now was! As well as a taste for irony. One must not forget that. Yes, one must not forget irony, in its most insidious sense, the ambiguous use of language to convey a privileged and corrupt meaning. (And how very different to the concept of irony that Nicolas was trying to master. Would one take precedence over the other?) Let the German masses believe about the purity of the Aryan race. It was the purity of his will to power that mattered most, channelled through the German people. Those who understood this understood Nazism. One couldn't *believe* in Nazism, one had to make something *of it*, a sharp instrument to get at history and make of it something Hitlerian. One had to stand back, and with an aristocratic regard, shape events to one's liking. This was the difference between a leader and his followers: The leader knew how *not* to take things seriously, how to be brutal (yes, even brutally honest, and the greatest of liars!), so as to keep sight of what is important, the pure Truth of his mission. This one had to take seriously, absolutely so. One had to know the difference between what to take seriously and what not to. Details no, but the Truth of Being, yes. One had to avoid getting lost in the petty concerns of the mass, in its need for reassurance and belief. The 'truth' of the many was not the issue, it was decisive action rooted in the Truth of the One that mattered most. The leader had to take upon himself a role detached from common human emotions, ready for the greatest comedy and the greatest pain. He must be the expression of the Truth of Being. He, Hitler, had to be inhuman so that Germans might discover the greatest within themselves, the greatest that humanity could offer. *There could be no forgiveness for everything weak.* No 'forgiveness' whatsoever, in any spiritual sense of the word.

First, Czechoslovakia. And the rest would follow. Better make friends of the Soviet beasts for the presents, and smash them later. France had to be taught a lesson. The Treaty of Versailles, with all the crippling effects it had had on Germany, demanded retribution. Hitler remembered his days as a corporal in the trenches, and his eyes assumed a glassy expression. Hard days, and not a thing to show for it. How much German blood had been spilt at Verdun and the Somme, only for Germany to finally be completely humiliated, not even allowed to retain her armies! It was in the trenches that his personality had been formed and hardened, after his pathetic attempts in Vienna at becoming a painter. No, this time it would be different. It was time for the German soul to sweep across continents! So it must be. So it would be. It was time that Germany made war on her enemies. Let the swastika fly, and the blood oaths be taken. The rest would follow.

Chapter 13:

Nietzsche's Dance

It is not our purpose to give an exhaustive explanation of Hitler, but rather to understand something of the motives of man in light of the influence he had on the events which concern us. We recall Marcel's observation, that Hitler had little sense of his own insignificance. I cannot agree more. Not only did Hitler have a theory about racial superiority which he claimed was the Truth about humanity, he believed himself to be the expression of the Truth of Being. *Hitler forgave reality nothing.*

Hitler used a species of irony to serve his own narcissism. He suffered from a blindness detrimental not only to his own health, but to the well-being of the world. Hitler saw himself as pure, unstoppable, Nietzschean will to power, Master of Forms. And yet Hitler could have done no greater injustice to the world of ideas. For if there was one thing that Nietzsche could not abide, it was the Truth of Being. Nietzsche describes reality as a dynamic movement of perspectives in which no one perspective has anything like a monopoly on Truth. Nietzsche's philosophy in fact turns out to be a very subtle theory of reality, as a mobile and conflictual affair where many truths compete for priority of place: a shadow-play. Nietzsche would not have denied that sugar is sweet. But he would have questioned our ability to get at anything like an absolute perspective on Sweetness, i.e. its Truth. In which case Hitler should have appreciated with greater subtlety the frailty of his own Truth. Sweet he was not.

An irony of history (in how may ways does irony come back to haunt us!): how a megalomaniac's dream hijacked the passionate vision of a destroyer of Truth.

Part Three:
<u>Contact</u>

As the shadow plays
So do we dance

Do not look for the shadow
Its unfolding is a mystery

Dare I speak of it?

Chapter 14
Point of Entry

Heidi stepped off of the train at the *Gare Austerlitz* in Paris. With the help of Gestapo intelligence, she had found a flat in *Le Marais,* in the 11th district. She quickly found her bearings, and took the metro to the appropriate station. She took the elevator in her building, and as she put the key in the lock to her door, she smiled discreetly. She would try to get her first glimpse of Garay tomorrow, at *La Scene*. It was Tuesday, and Gestapo intelligence was informed that every Wednesday Garay met there with Gilbert Marcel.

Her flat, a one-bedroom, was on the fifth floor, with a magnificent view. Heidi undressed, took a bath, and sat at the kitchen table. She took a deep breath, opened the dossier on Garay, and perused its contents. Her plan was to go to *La Scene,* and observe Garay before trying to connect with him. Once again, she liked what she saw in the dossier. Garay had an animal presence about him which she found intriguing. She suspected that inside the polished man lay a vitality and thirst for life, a passion for achievement, that could throw itself against the greatest of obstacles.

Heidi had brought two weapons with her: a stiletto, and a pistol. Over a period of months, Klaus had taught her how to use both. He had also taught her commando-style physical combat: direct and lethal. Heidi took the weapons out of her suitcase, stripped the gun and cleaned it, checked the magazine, and set the weapon aside. She put on loose-fitting clothes. Moving the living-room furniture against the wall, she now used the resulting space to stretch, and then to perform the movements essential to physical combat, slowly at first, and then at realistic speed, first with the stiletto, and then without it. She breathed deeply and regularly, as she had been taught, and focussed her mind on the present. She felt ready. She would take a nap, and then go to the *musee Rodin* where she would seek inspiration in the extraordinary movement of stone.

Chapter 15
La Scene 1

Heidi arrived at *La Scene* at mid-afternoon, the time of day when Garay met with Gilbert Marcel. She positioned herself so that she had a view of most of the tables. The majority of them were taken. She saw neither Garay nor Marcel. Ordering a coffee, she took out a book, and set about waiting for the arrival of the two men.

About a quarter of an hour after Heidi's arrival, Garay and Marcel made their entry. They sat three tables away from Heidi. At this distance, Heidi got her first view of Garay in the flesh, and she was not disappointed. He radiated the energy and charisma that she had seen in the photographs. Marcel exuded an intense and focussed energy. The two men were deep in conversation, and spoke discreetly, in low tones. Heidi could not say what they were talking about. And so she set about observing Garay's body language.

Garay's gestures were minimalist. He used his hands to emphasize or explain a point, and his facial expressions indicated an acute awareness of his environment. His legs were crossed, and he leaned back into his chair. He had about him an air of focus and equilibrium. He would make an interesting target. Not a man to be taken lightly.

Heidi pretended to read, and continued to study Garay. Suddenly their eyes met, and Garay gave her a charming smile. Heidi smiled back. She knew immediately, then, that her mission had the potential to be a success. Garay had reacted with pleasure, as was expected, to her beauty. The next step would be to see what he thought of her as a German.

<u>Chapter 16</u>
La Scene 2

Heidi signed up for Marcel's course, and immediately approached him in person. He was charming and helpful. Over the course of a month, they met three times briefly to discuss the reading material. That was enough, thought Heidi. Enough to permit a hello at *La Scene*, and, hopefully, to be introduced to Garay.

***

Heidi sat at *La Scene*, waiting for Garay and Marcel to arrive. She had chosen a table right next to where they usually sat. As usual, she had a book with her, which she pretended to read. When the two men arrived, and seated themselves, she did not look up immediately, but continued to read her book. She hoped that Marcel would recognise her. And so she sat, legs crossed, and waited.

After fifteen minutes or so, not having had the reaction from Marcel that she had hoped for, Heidi got up from her chair. She got up slowly, and caught Marcel's eye. Having decided to initiate the meeting, Heidi smiled, and stretched her hand out in greeting.

'How are you, professor Marcel?', she asked.

'Very well, Heidi', responded Marcel. 'And you?'

'Well, thank you.'

'Allow me to introduce a friend of mine, Jean Garay. Jean, this is Heidi Braun, a student of mine.'

'Good to meet you', said Garay. He gave Heidi a purposeful look, and continued, 'Would you care to join us?'

'With pleasure,' replied Heidi, and she sat at the table with the two men, opposite to Garay, who gave her a winning smile.

'You are German. How are you enjoying life in Paris?', asked Garay. 'Is it everything you hoped for?'

'So far, yes' replied Heidi. 'Paris is a beautiful city, and I'm happy to be able to study here. And I've had the good chance to have enrolled in professor Marcel's course, which is very interesting. It's also good to be out of Germany. I'm not terribly impressed with Nazism.'

'Well, it's certainly good to hear a German express that sentiment,' said Garay. 'How long do you expect to stay in Paris?'

'I'm not sure yet. At least a year, perhaps two. It all depends on how my studies progress. I would like to stay as long as I can. I'm in no rush to get back to Germany.'

'Out of interest, what do you think will happen in Germany?', asked Garay. 'Some fear that war is imminent. Do you share that sentiment?'

'I really don't know,' replied Heidi. 'Certainly, the fact that Germany has rebuilt her armies is a telling sign. But I really don't know. What do you think?'

'Oh, I don't know. But there is some concern in France that Hitler means to wage war. Anyway, it's a dull subject for a beautiful woman such as yourself..'

Heidi smiled. 'Thank you for the compliment. I'm flattered'

'Not at all,' said Garay. 'The truth speaks for itself.'

'Indeed', said Marcel.

'Thank you both. You're quite charming. Well, gentlemen, I will leave you now. Good to talk to you both. Hope to do it again soon.'

The two men stood and shook Heidi's hand in turn. She left them both. She had established contact with Garay. A decisive move in the dance of seduction …

Chapter 17
Shadow Warriors

The way a woman moves speaks of her desire. And so did Heidi move, a cunning sentiment enfolded in German beauty. And her desire was calculated to achieve a defined end, an open wound in the flesh of her prey, a flowing out of information and knowledge.

If Garay had a weakness, it was for feminine beauty. But he had always chosen easy prey, women he could use and then discard. But with Heidi, whom he had indeed taken as his mistress, he had made a gross miscalculation. She, of course, hid from him her true nature and intent.

***

Let us not think that the hero of our story was as naïve as we might suppose. And I am speaking here of Nicolas. For Nicolas, as much as he wondered about reality, metaphysics, and the world, was also a ninja. He had trained with some of the most hardened ninjas in Paris, and also in Japan. He had learned how to kill, with and without weapons. He had an intimate knowledge of Zen philosophy adapted to the martial arts. He also had an intimate knowledge of firearms, stealth, espionage, and an interest in combat telepathy. He was as much a warrior as he was a philosopher and writer. *Above all, he was an individual.*

Interlude

It may seem strange today for an author to intervene in the the midst of his story-telling to speak directly to his readers. I do so now at my own peril. But I see a need for the concept of authorship, of the individual, essentially, to be held up for scrutiny. For, in my estimation, language is in grave danger of slipping into the pointless anarchy that we call 'postmodernism,' where the author, in nihilistic fashion, forces upon the reader a dubious narrative: a condition that we might call 'subjectivism'. Why subjectivism? Because the author, or what is left of him, does as he pleases. Why 'dubious'? Because there are no stable points of reference, and the author claims to lose himself in the very anarchy he writes about. The 'individual', as such, is lost - on all levels (apparently the writer falls into some sort of schizophrenic malaise, and as such is 'postmodern.' I'm not quite sure. I dare not ask, 'who's there?').

I too for many years slumbered in the 'flat' abstraction of 'deconstruction' (and there is a system there, you know - in the *continuity* of the style writing. And much insight. And trickery. And most importantly, a lack of understanding amongst Derrida's interpreters. He is not *quite* 'postmodern'. He is an individual, a great intellect. But too flat in his approach*: a bottomless chessboard.* And to that extent, he gives over too large a part of his identity to postmodernism; *insofar, that is, as he too often resists conceding positive points of reference.* What about a poem, Jacques?) There is no doubt in my mind that my turn to deconstruction was fuelled by an adolescent longing for freedom from the world in which I grew up, a world of strong men and women. I *used* deconstruction to redirect and blunt the ruthless barbs of Religion, Law and History that characterised my captivity. And I succeeded in avoiding apotheosis. And for that I give thanks.

Make no mistake: from the point of view of intellectual battle, deconstruction is a very effective weapon. But more than that I do not see. After having read many of Derrida's books, having defended them in fierce encounters, and having immersed my psyche in Heidegger in order to get at Derrida, I now find truth and solace in fiction and poetry: in writings, that is, which offer the reader a wider expanse and depth of interpretation and feeling, *but with the author in mind.* And his/her unconscious too, if need be. Let's stick with

Freud, shall we. The writing is really quite beautiful, and the train of thought wonderfully lucid. Especially the accuracy of his critique of civilisation. Or should we fall prey yet again to philosophy's latest fashion?

Let us take Picasso's *Guernica* as a point of departure, a work which we encountered briefly in chapter five. We characterised *Guernica* as a montage of *'screams and disembodied voices with distorted faces. Not voices, really. More like tonalities bringing to mind archetypal spirits. Dark places full of destruction and perversity. An edge cutting endlessly into reality. A sexual grimace lost somewhere in the folds of severed flesh. A hacking, piercing, exploding truth to it all ... a play of shadow and light ... a sign, perhaps, of things to come.'*

What Picasso is patently doing in this painting is bringing to light the awful reality of war, and the unconscious forces which drive it. This is one man's vision of things, *insofar as he interprets reality.* It is the work of an immensely strong and talented artistic mind. *It is the work of one man,* whatever the archetypal complexity of the situation which he painted. A man who was able to reach into the human psyche to show the atrocities it is capable of. The work is

Freudian to that extent: it shows us what we are, or can be, *as individuals,* when our destructive instincts take hold.

Of course, Freud diagnosed the psyche of the individual as a complex interplay of forces. As consisting, in effect, in three parts: the unconscious, the ego, and the super-ego. The super-ego places the individual in touch with a collective consciousness, which moulds the timelessness of the unconscious, structuring thought and feeling in space and time, with ethical imperatives in mind. The ego is our personal identity, haunted by the unconscious, and tamed by the super-ego. So where does that leave us, what with our emphasis on the individual? Is the individual a complex monad (as it is in ego psychology), or a more fully social being? We must *doubly affirm* (Derrida, thanks: very important) the individual as both singular and social, a complex interaction of forces both internal and external.

And yet: Being an individual is about forging one's own destiny, one's mind, in the face of chaos, destruction, and pointless vulgarity (yes, I am a modernist - with love and respect for *some* women). As Thomas Mann put it: 'a man [or woman] who is capable of achievement over and above the average and expected modicum must be equipped either with a moral remoteness and single-mindedness which is rare indeed and of heroic mould, or else with an exceptionally robust vitality'. What I am attempting in this novella is to reach out to such 'robust' minds, male and female, to study their different reactions to the same historical situation, *as they interact as social individuals in the world*. I do not think Mann would disagree with Marx when the latter said: 'men make history, but not in circumstances of their own choosing.' Indeed, Mann also writes '[a] man lives not only his personal life, as an individual, but also, consciously or unconsciously, the life of his epoch and his contemporaries.'

So the individual exists always in a situation, *but as an individual*. 'The dream is over', said Husserl about the transcendental ego. Perhaps he spoke too soon. We are still, after all, waiting for Nietzsche's *ubermenschen*. (Forgive the rather loose affiliation between Husserl and Nietzsche: but is not aristocratic detachment an important theme for both? Getting beyond base vulgarity and all that ….). I suspect that Nietzsche's strong individuals shall in no way resemble Hitler, as much as higher, more enlightened, *fully social* beings with an aristocratic regard (not necessarily *of* aristocratic heritage); and, importantly, with a developed sense of forgiveness, albeit one that is purposeful and capable of ruthless intervention. The evolution of the human race? Are we already there? But that is a matter for philosophical and scientific debate.

One last word: about the relationship between shadow and evil. We often use the term 'shadow' to define everything that is not good, that escapes the good. This is not my intention in this novel. 'Shadow-play' as defined by Marcel coincides with Richard's argument that, insofar as we cannot aspire to be entirely good, we must accept that we are all, to this extent, evil. All human beings are evil *We are all sinners*. We all exist as shadows of the good, as shadows across water. It is a question of staying in touch, however, with the good in what Richard describes as 'movements of transcendence'. In these movements we find God's forgiveness for being partial creatures *capable of spiritual development.*

But all of that is perhaps still too abstract, even if it must have a place in our thinking. There is a further aspect to evil which I shall call 'The Event'. This is a more thoroughly existential approach to the problem of evil, where evil reflects on itself, and rather than reaching out to the good for forgiveness, seeks destruction for its own sake. It ceases to communicate with the good (in any form.) 'The Event' has no place in shadow-play. It is pure, narcissistic self-affirmation. We might speak of the 'Hitler Event'. 'The Event' lies waiting in the deepest recesses of the psyche, in the timeless movement of the unconscious, *whence it becomes conscious*, and is acted upon in utter detachment.

And, that said, let us now return to our story, spy story and novel of ideas, as it aspires to be, simultaneously (or better, as a weave).

Part Four:
The Turning

The turning escapes analysis.
Here we discover language within language
Gesture and the spoken word mingle,
Passion and boredom pull at each other

In the heat of war
Hearts and minds fall prey to ambiguity
What seems sure is rendered uncertain
By the turning

In the turning we find the very soul
Of what is spiritual ...
Players haunted by the inevitable
Wishing for Eternity's wisdom

Our story unfolds in the turning
It is called to reality by the turning ...
And the turning is a shadow-play

Chapter 18
Subterfuge

In May of 1940, Germany's armies swept through France, pushing out of the Ardennes, avoiding the Maginot Line and sweeping French and British armies into the sea at Dunkirk in a classic *blitzkrieg* manoeuvre, using heavy armour to pierce lines of resistance, surround and destroy them.

France lay divided. The Germans occupied the north, the French, under the Vichy regime, the south. The war raged on in Europe. There were those who sought to resist the German occupation of France from within (De Gaulle leading the Free French abroad). Among them were the players in our story: Nicolas, Richard, Jean Garay, Gilbert Marcel and Katya.

***

Our group of players called itself **'Lucifer's Tooth'**. Its *raison d'etre* was to get pilots who had been shot down out of

France and back to Britain. It was decided that the pilots be taken to the Basque country, where Garay had the necessary connections to ensure safe passage. There were spies everywhere. It was necessary to find a strip of land where a small two-seater plane could land in secrecy, and take the pilot back to Britain. Or to take a path over the Pyrenees into Spain.

***

And where was Heidi in all of this? She was, thus far, oblivious to Lucifer's Tooth. Garay considered her a mistress, and as such not relevant to his work in the resistance. But Heidi was not to be put off. With a warrior's intuition, she sensed that something was afoot. But how was she to gain the confidence and trust of Garay? She and Klaus decided that there was only one way to do so: to feign betrayal of her own country. To become, in effect, a double-agent.

Chapter nineteen
Tactics and Strategy

The strategy of Lucifer's Tooth was to get downed flyers safely out of France. After much debate and discussion, it was decided, from a tactical perspective, that Katya and Richard would be fully active, ready at a moment's notice to do what was necessary; that Marcel would stay on in Paris and continue teaching, ready to pass information if called upon; that Garay would go to the Basque country; and that Nicolas would move in secret between Paris and the Basque country, and elsewhere in France, cultivating and consolidating contacts between different members of the Resistance, which was a highly dispersed effort. Nicolas would go by the codename 'Wolf'. The other members of the group would recognise each other by the password Lucifer.

***

Having consulted with Klaus, Heidi approached Garay, and told him that she had been approached by the Gestapo, asking her to seduce him, and gather information. In effect, she told him the truth, turning it to her own advantage. She suggested that she should indeed take on the position of seductress, and wary of Nazism, she told Garay, she would like to help him in whatever way possible.

Garay immediately saw the possibility of feeding the Gestapo misleading information. The question was, should he let Heidi into his confidence?

After much deliberation within the team, it was agreed that Heidi should be tested over a period of time to ensure that what she was telling was the truth; that she would not be given the password, Lucifer's Tooth; and that her only contact within the group would be Garay. Heidi's job would be to liase with the Gestapo, feeding them false information, and that was all she would do for the time being. Until, that is, she proved herself, at which time she would be given full status in the group.

Chapter Twenty
A Magician's Tale

Nicolas stepped off the train onto the platform in Bordeaux. He was was to make contact with members of a Resistance group. This was not the first time he was doing so. Indeed, Nicolas had been operating now the better part of six months. Word had been spread within the resistance of an operator named Wolf, and that his password was Lucifer.

And what can we say about Nicolas as we observe him walking to his destination? Shall we tell a magician's tale? A complex man, no doubt, someone who sought to live life in all its more interesting aspects. His position now was especially complex. Here he was, a philosopher thinking about the Truth, and then suddenly the winds of war had blown him off course. This did not mean that he had to cease to think like a philosopher, but that there were other priorities at hand. What Nicolas did carry with him as an operator was his deep appreciation of purity, his understanding of 'forgiveness', and his love of irony.

Ninjutsu had taught Nicolas to detach himself from his emotions. Or better, how to channel them so as to have a maximum effect when in contact with the enemy. Psychologically, he was prepared for the worst. He would have to move like the wind, become a shadow, adopt a magician's posture if he were to play and win this game of espionage.

So far Nicolas had participated in the escape of two flyers, who, with the help of Garay, had flown out of the Basque country. The work had proved very dangerous. The gestapo were everywhere. Two German soldiers on patrol had been liquidated. Nicolas had been prepared to kill, if necessary; and indeed he had slit the throat of one of the two Germans. Nicolas had never killed before, but he sensed that that this would not be the last time. This was going to be hard magic.

Having made contact with his fellow resistance members, Nicolas was told that there was a flyer in hiding in the north of France, close to Strasbourg, and that the Germans were doing their best to track him down. Immediate action was required.

***

Having been preoccupied in the field, Nicolas decided that he would go through Paris on his way to Strasbourg. He had not seen Katya for many months, and he missed her company.

When he arrived at Katya's apartment, he found Heidi there. Their first reaction to each other was that of two strong individuals attempting to gauge the strength of the other. Katya quickly explained to Nicolas that Heidi had gone to ground, and why.

Nicolas was struck by Heidi's beauty, but this was less important to him than the presence she projected, which gave the impression of strength and resilience. He could not know that they would one day meet under very different circumstances.

For her part, Heidi felt a curious kinship with Nicolas, a sense of freedom and possibility that she had not shared with many men. She felt drawn to him. Like Nicolas, she did not know that they were fated, for better or worse.

Chapter 21
Untruth

There is no Truth, but there are untruths. Heidi, after consultation with the Gestapo, had already created a number of scenarios to prove to Garay that she could be trusted. The gestapo had given her, for example, lists of names of people who they suspected of sympathizing with the resistance. When Garay asked her how she got the information, she told him that her ranking was high enough in the gestapo to have access to privileged information.

The latest move had been the most impressive. The gestapo had arranged for Heidi to relay the information to Garay that they would seek to capture a member of the resistance hiding in Paris. Heidi provided Garay with a name and address.

Garay took the necessary steps to forewarn the hunted man. And the gestapo did indeed raid his hiding place. And they did so with full knowledge that they would find nothing. Still wary of betrayal, Garay was nonetheless impressed with the consistency with which Heidi's information played itself out.

***

The crucial moment arrived when Heidi told Garay that she had been held for questioning be the gestapo, and that she feared for her life. She needed to go into hiding. She and Klaus had decided that infiltration into Lucifer's Tooth was essential. Contact with Garay was not good enough. The gestapo needed to identify the other members of the group, and to do so, Heidi would have to go deep undercover. Her codename would be Frega.

Garay, after further deliberation with the group, decided that Heidi could be trusted, so far as the situation dictated. She had proved herself several times over, and if her life was in danger, then she needed protection. Richard asked British intelligence to run a check on her, and she came up clean. She would be put up by Katya for the time being. She was still not told about Lucifer's Tooth.

***

The gestapo had learnt, through their own intelligence networks, of a resistance operation, Lucifer's Tooth, and of an operator code-named Wolf who was doing significant liaison work between resistance groups. The word was that he was highly sophisticated, and that his work within the resistance was to get downed flyers out of France.

Klaus met with Heidi, and told her that her new mission was to identify Wolf, and neutralise him. It was suspected that he had close ties with Garay. Through Heidi's efforts, the gestapo knew now of three members of Lucifer's Tooth, a group which they recognised by affiliation (not knowing that the three were indeed members of Lucifer's Tooth): Garay, Katya, and Nicolas, and decided to leave them be, in the hope that they might lead them to Lucifer's Tooth, and to Wolf. Richard and Marcel remained unknown to the gestapo.

Chapter 22
The Hunt

The hunt for Wolf was on. Lucifer's Tooth had confirmation from other resistance groups that capturing Wolf was high on the agenda of the gestapo. The resistance had shown a remarkable degree of success in getting downed flyers out of France and over to England; and the gestapo was determined to stem the tide.

***

As he made his way to Strasbourg, Nicolas reflected on the man he had killed. He felt genuine sorrow. He hated this war. And yet, he had fast become deeply involved in it. How then was he to manage his sorrrow and reticence? He reflected on the nature of 'forgiveness' as he had come to understand it, and about the play of shadows which Marcel had shared with him as an explanation for human nature. He did not hate the Germans, even less so the ones he must kill. Being would decide their ultimate fate. There was a savage war on, and Nicolas prayed to Being to guide him in his work, and to forgive him for his actions, and those of the Germans.

Did he have to kill that German, who had been patrolling the area where a flyer was preparing to leave for England? Yes, it had had to be done. And it had been done in the way of the ninja. Nicolas had said a brief prayer over the body of the dead German, that he may find Being. And indeed, Nicolas knew that in order to keep going, to keep escaping the gestapo, who he knew were after him, to keep killing, he would have to become the consummate warrior. He must detach himself from his emotions, and get the job done. He must become shadow conscious of itself, invisible to all, even Katya. This did not mean that he was abandoning Lucifer's Tooth, but that he was preparing himself mentally and emotionally for the difficult events of the future. He must be solid as the earth, fluid as water, winged like the wind, and as ferocious as fire. These were the four elements of ninjutsu, Zen Buddhist philosophy: earth, water, wind and fire. But Nicolas knew that ultimately, if he was to survive, he would have to become like the void, the most sophisticated state of being of Zen. And this meant cutting himself off from his emotions. In the void there is no evil.

Nicolas had taken the codename 'Wolf' in memory of his dream about Christ and the wolf. He was animal, Christ the god. The god who promised purity for those seeking it. And the void, as expressed in ninjutsu, was also a meditation on purity. In fact, what both Christ and the ninja had in common was the ability to experience moments of transcendence, Christ in his love, and the ninja in the void.

***

A breakthrough came the gestapo's way. They had captured members of a resistance group, and under interrogation and torture, had acquired a description of Wolf.

Upon receiving a copy of the description, Heidi immediately recognised Nicolas. The priority was to capture Wolf. And if there were other members of Lucifer's Tooth, besides Katya and Garay, their identities would be revealed under interrogation and torture.

***

Nicolas was not in the dark. He had been in touch with Garay, who informed him that the secrecy of Lucifer's tooth had been compromised. There was constant surveillance of both him and Katya, and Heidi. The only thing to do was to go further underground. And to take Katya and Heidi with him. The two women left Paris on different trains, and upon arriving in the Basque Country, were immediately inserted into Basque homes high in the mountains.

As for Richard and Marcel, who had both, in one way or the other had participated in Lucifer's Tooth, (for example, by passing information along), it was decided that they too should go underground. The danger of their capture now was great. So they too went into hiding in the Basque country. And it goes without saying that Nicolas joined the group. His identity had been compromised, and it was imperative that he go into hiding. Garay's wife and children went also into hiding.

And so we find the players in our story in hiding in the mountains. They had managed to get three flyers out of France safely. But little known to them was that Heidi, alias Frega, was a spy. And that she would do her best to deliver them to the gestapo.

But it wasn't to be as easy as all that. The group had split up, and with the help of a resistance group already established in the Basque Country, had done so so that no one of them knew where the others were. So should one be caught, the identity and location of the others would not be compromised. Each member of the group was armed with a pistol, a commando knife, and a sten machine gun, and taught how to use them.

****

What was the group to do now that they had been dispersed, and gone into hiding? Garay, for his part, was not in favour of doing nothing but hide from the Germans. He consequently sent messages through secure channels that the group should continue their work, but remain in the mountains. It was decided that the best way to proceed, would be for the entire group to stay in hiding in the Basque Country, merging with the resistance already operating in the region. Garay was well inserted into the Basque elements of the resistance. Nicolas had contacts around the country, Richard was still in communication with British Intelligence. Marcel, Katya and Heidi were on hand, available if need be.

***

Heidi was deep undercover, and was not sure what to do. All movement was watched by the resistance, especially where those in hiding were in particular danger. How would she make contact with the gestapo? It was now known that Wolf was in the Pyrenees, and Heidi had confirmed that information. But she knew neither where he was, nor whether she would ever see him again. And in a way, she was glad to be in the position in which she found herself. For some unknown reason, she hoped that Wolf would escape capture and/or death. Indeed, after their brief meeting in Paris, she felt a deep affinity with him, though little did she know of him. As for Garay, he had been too busy to spend much time with Heidi. She accepted this. And at any rate, her new orders were to neutralise the Wolf. What was she to do?

Chapter 23
Frega & the Wolf

Garay went to see Nicolas. He had just spoken with Richard, and British Intelligence had informed him that Heidi was indeed a gestapo agent, codenamed Frega. Garay's first impulse was to have her shot. But Nicolas thought differently. He suggested that he talk with Heidi, and confront her with the fact that her cover was blown. And so it was decided.

***

It was a beautifully clear day in the mountains, sun shining off snow, as Nicolas walked with a guide towards his confrontation with Heidi. Nicolas had no weapon with him. They finally arrived at a house high in the pyrennees, cut off from civilisation.

Nicolas knocked on the door, and it was opened by an old, wizened Basque woman. Heidi sat at the kitchen table, drinking a cup of coffee. Nicolas was once again struck by the force of her presence.

'Hello, Heidi, how are you?' said Nicolas.

'Fine , and you?' she responded.

'I'm well. Listen, we need to talk. Would you care to go for a walk?'

'Yes, I'd love to.'

***

Nicolas and Heidi walked on a path which took them further up into the mountains. The guide followed somewhere behind.

Nicolas got straight to the point.

'We have proof from British Intelligence that you are still, and always have been, working for the gestapo. What do you have to say about these allegations?'

Heidi took a long time to respond. Then she replied, 'Yes, it's true. Will you shoot me now?'

'No, against the wishes of Garay, I will not shoot you. You are a foolish young woman, with considerable talent and a strong personality; but considering the fact that you did very little damage to Lucifer's Tooth, even if you might have liked to, your presence in our group was relatively benign, thanks to the secrecy with which we operate. And more to the point, I believe you were manipulated by the gestapo. Your sense of adventure, if I am right on this, got the better of you.'

'So you are free to go. My guide will take you to a place where you can easily contact the German authorities. If you show your face around here ever again, you will be shot on sight. Understood?'

'Yes'.

Heidi felt overwhelmed. Her mission had failed. She took a last look at Nicolas, at his eyes full of expression, and she felt a deep pain inside. She could have loved this man. Delicately, she kissed him on the cheek, and turned and walked away.

***

Nicolas sat alone with a bottle of whiskey. It seemed such a long time ago that he had talked to Marcel and Richard about shadows, forgiveness and transcendence. It had been several months since he had released Heidi to her fate. He knew he had done the right thing. She had simply been a naïve young woman taken advantage of by the gestapo. He had little contact with Marcel, who had retreated into his books. Richard had gone underground in France, and sometimes Nicolas ran into him on a mission. And although he still loved Katya, he saw little of her what with all the moving about that he did. But she was alive and well, hidden in the mountains. Garay was still operating a Basque resistance movement.

He looked at the glass of whiskey in front of him, and saw all the hatred and violence of war of which he had been, and still was, a part. The Germans were being pushed back on all fronts, but the fighting was still intense. How many had he killed?

And, so it seemed, there it was: blood, mutilation and gore, and philosophy be damned. Until time called forth another turning.

THE END